This Little Tiger book
belongs to:

D0177100

For Eriko Arikawa McGee and our Japanese family – especially Mitsuyuki, Kazuko and Mitsuko ~ M M

For my sister Susan R Macnaughton ~ T M

LITTLE TIGER PRESS
An imprint of Magi Publications
1 The Coda Centre, 189 Munster Road, London SW6 6AW
www.littletigerpress.com

First published in Great Britain 2006
This edition published 2006

A CIP catalogue record for this book is available from the British Library

 • ISBN 1 84506 264 7

Printed in China

10 9 8 7 6 5 4 3 2 1

While Angels Watch

Marni McGee   Tina Macnaughton

LITTLE TIGER PRESS
London

Long ago, when the world was new,
The Angels all had work to do.
They picked the colours of the dawn,
Clouds of pink and skies of blue.

Some taught dolphins how to swim,
To dance in sparkling seas . . .
Diving down with silvery fish,
Then leaping up with playful ease.

Some showed spiders how to spin
And helped them hang their webs in trees.
The smallest Angels of them all
Painted stripes on bumblebees.

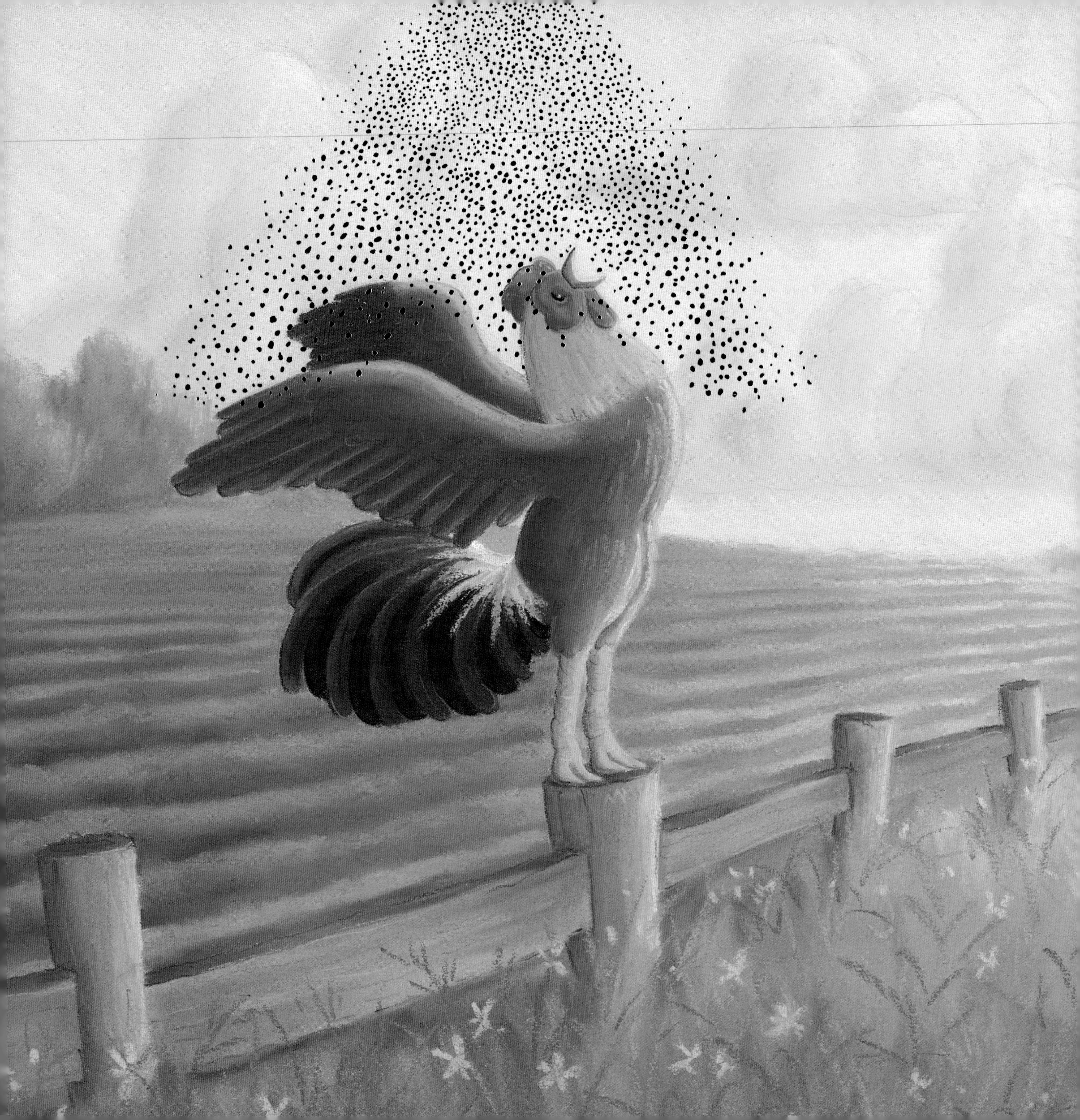

Other Angels told the roosters
Where to perch and when to crow.
But where did all those Angels go?
Where are they now? Does no one know?

"I've heard," said Lamb, "that once they came
To sing a newborn baby's birth.
The hillside glowed with Angels' light.
I wonder, are they still on Earth?"

"The Angels are still here," said Owl.
"They teach our babies how to sing.
They show us how to nest and fly,
To sail the sky on silent wing."

"Once," said Calf, "I wandered off –
Far from mother, far from hay.
I could not find my cosy barn
Until an Angel showed the way."

"I heard Angels," murmured Dog.
"On the day my pups were born.
As each one raised its tiny head,
A joyful Angel blew her horn."

"I've seen Angels play," said Hare.
"They race with Fox and dark-eyed Deer.
And when a whispering river speaks,
Angels gather close to hear."

"But what of children?" wondered Duck.
"They have no feathers, have no fur.
Could Angels care for *them* as well?
They cannot fly nor even purr!"

"The Angels love each one," said Cat.
"I've watched and know it's true.
Angels hover round by day
To guide in all that children do."

"And I have seen with my green eyes:
At night the Angels guard their beds.
The children sleep with happy dreams
When gentle Angels touch their heads."

More magical books from Little Tiger Press

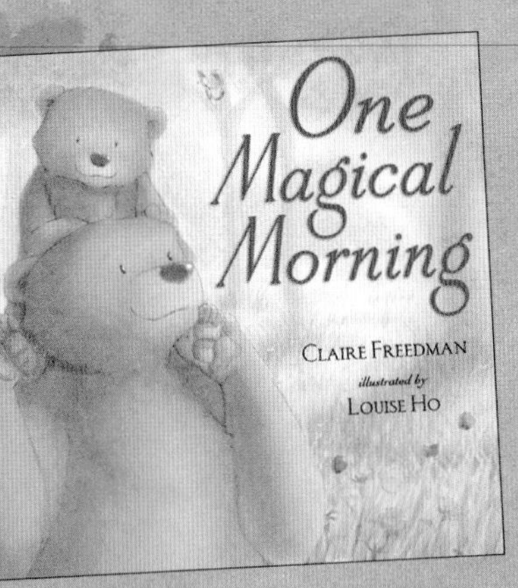

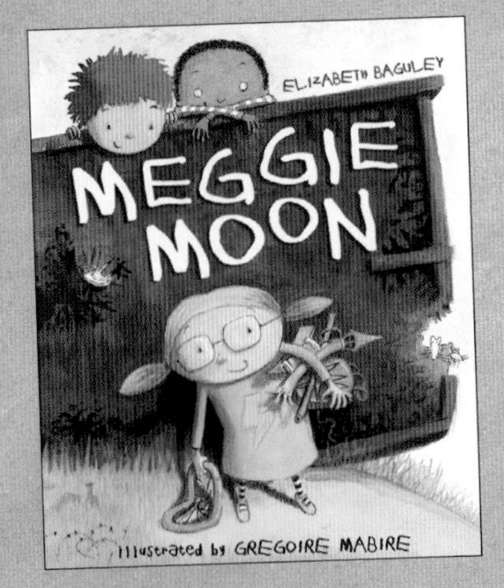

For information regarding any of the above titles
or for our catalogue, please contact us:
Little Tiger Press, 1 The Coda Centre,
189 Munster Road, London SW6 6AW
Tel: 020 7385 6333 Fax: 020 7385 7333
E-mail: info@littletiger.co.uk
www.littletigerpress.com